GUBBIX
THE POISON FISH

With special thanks to Brandon Robshaw

For Jericho Aiken

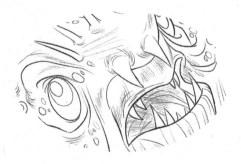

www.beastquest.co.uk

ORCHARD BOOKS

First published in Great Britain in 2014 by Orchard Books
This edition published in 2018 by The Watts Publishing Group

3 5 7 9 10 8 6 4

Text © 2014 Beast Quest Limited.
Cover and inside illustrations by Artful Doodlers with special thanks to Bob and Justin
© Orchard Books 2014

Beast Quest is a registered trademark of Beast Quest Limited
Series created by Beast Quest Limited, London

A CIP catalogue record for this book is available from the British Library.

ISBN 978 1 40832 867 5

Printed in Great Britain by Clays Ltd, St Ives plc

The paper and board used in this book are made from wood from responsible sources

Orchard Books
An imprint of Hachette Children's Group
Part of The Watts Publishing Group Limited
Carmelite House, 50 Victoria Embankment, London EC4Y 0DZ

An Hachette UK Company
www.hachette.co.uk
www.hachettechildrens.co.uk

GUBBIX
THE POISON FISH

BY ADAM BLADE

ORCHARD

I'm coming for you, Max!

You think you have defeated me - the mighty Cora Blackheart? Idiot boy! You've only made me angry! I may have lost my ship and my crew, but it's not over. Now it's just you and me...and the deadly Robobeasts under my control!

You have something that I want, Max - an object so powerful, I can use it to rule all of Nemos! And you don't even know it...

But first I will destroy your whole family - your mother, your father...and that irritating Merryn girl, too.

Cora Blackheart will have her revenge!

CHAPTER ONE

BATTLE STATIONS

Way up at the top of a lighthouse, Max sat in the seat of a giant telescope, staring through the eyepiece at the glittering blue water of the Lost Lagoon. The roof of the lighthouse was open, allowing the telescope to sweep the whole way round so that Max could view the Lagoon from all sides.

It was an amazingly powerful telescope. Max could see all the islands as far as the horizon. But what held his attention was

the figure of Cora Blackheart, the villainous
pirate, riding an aquabike across the water,
straight towards them. He could see her in
close-up, framed in the circular lens. Her
hair blew in the breeze like a nest of snakes.

Max felt his heartbeat speed up. "We don't
have long," he said, without taking his eye
from the telescope. He knew that his friend

Lia, his dogbot Rivet and the old lighthouse-keeper, Piscanias, were all waiting anxiously behind him. "Cora's on her way. Let's get out of here!"

"Let me see!" Lia said, nudging him. Lia's home city had been attacked by a robotically enhanced beast in the past – the fearsome Cephalox. Max knew she was desperate to escape from this Lagoon and warn her people that Cora was at large, and could attack with another Robobeast. Max slipped out of the seat to let Lia take her turn. She glued her face to the eyepiece.

"Right, it's time for you lot to leave," the grizzled old lighthouse-keeper said. "I don't want to be dragged into your mess."

"Don't worry," Max said. "We don't want to hang around either!"

The door burst open and Max's mum, Niobe, rushed in. She was panting hard, and clutching a round metal object.

The compass, Max thought. It looked like his mum had almost finished constructing it.

"Have you seen?" she gasped. "Cora's on her way! We need some Barrum, and fast."

Max nodded, trying to keep calm. The compass was made out of Galdium, Rullium and Fennum so far, but they needed a fourth and last metal, Barrum, before it would work properly.

"My compass looked a lot better than that," said Piscanias, a little sniffily. "But yes – a Barrum needle is all you need. Then you can use the compass to escape from the Lost Lagoon and leave me in peace."

Lia moved away from the telescope, her face anxious. "She's almost here!"

"Do you know where we can get some Barrum?" Max asked Piscanias again.

"No!" snapped the lighthouse-keeper, scowling. He seemed to think for a moment. "Well, I suppose you could try the Underwater Market. They sell all kinds of things there."

"How do we get there?" Max asked.

Piscanias pointed through the lighthouse window. "See that small island of black rock, straight ahead?"

Max looked through the telescope again. The island swam into view. "Yes."

"Make for that. When you get there, turn left. Keep going, and after a while, you'll see some metal pillars sticking up through the sea. That's the site of the Underwater Market. Now will you go, please? I don't like company."

"Right," said Max, committing the directions to memory. "Thanks, Piscanias, and sorry to trouble you." *Though we did save your lighthouse from a flock of nasty birds*, he thought. "Anyway, don't worry, Cora won't attack your lighthouse. It's us she's after!"

Max took the compass from Niobe and shoved it in his pocket. Then he nodded at the others and ran from the room, down the spiral staircase. He heard them clattering down behind him. They came out into the open air, where the *Leaping Dolphin* stood

on the quayside.

Rivet was waiting for them, running up and down in excitement. Spike, Lia's pet swordfish, jumped from the water, his round eyes gazing up at Lia. She bent down and stroked his head.

"All right, boy," she said. "We're on our way, and soon we'll be out of this Lagoon!"

"Goodbye, and good riddance!" said Piscanias, and slammed the lighthouse door.

Max looked out to sea. Even without the telescope, Cora was visible now, an approaching dot in the ocean trailed by a white wake.

Max's mother took a remote control device from her tunic and pointed it at the *Leaping Dolphin*. There was a whirr and a click, and caterpillar tracks suddenly slid out of the bottom of the sub. It swiftly moved forwards and slid into the water.

"Hey, that's clever!" Lia said.

She must be really impressed, Max thought. Lia didn't think much of technology.

"Yes, it's not a bad little feature," Niobe said modestly. She clicked the remote again and the sub's hatch slid open. "Everybody in! Then it's goodbye, Cora."

The sunlight glinted on the green brooch

Niobe wore pinned to her tunic.

Cora would love to get her hands on that, Max thought. The brooch gave the wearer the power to control any person or beast. And suddenly, Max had a brilliant idea. He was sick of being terrorised by Cora. Sick of running from her. It was time to make a stand.

"Wait!" he said. "Why don't we take her on? We'll never have a better chance. The *Leaping Dolphin* is at full power. Cora doesn't have a Robobeast with her. And we've got the green brooch – we can use it to control her mind!"

There was a moment's silence.

"You're right!" Lia said, smashing her fist into her palm. "I'm fed up with that Breather chasing us around. Let's teach her a lesson!"

Niobe nodded, slowly. "It makes sense," she said. "But we have to be careful. That pirate doesn't play fair."

"Sandwiches!" barked Rivet excitedly. Then, in a soft, whining voice, he said "Sandwiches" again. Max felt sorry for him. The dogbot's speech circuits were scrambled, and "sandwiches" was the only word he could say. He was clearly getting tired of it.

"Don't worry, Riv," Max said. "I'll fix you up – as soon as we've defeated Cora!"

Max, Lia and Rivet climbed through the hatch of the submarine and slid into their seats. Niobe came in last and locked the hatch behind them. The control panel hummed into life and a hundred little lights flashed on as she pressed the starter button.

The sub surged through the water in Cora's direction. It darkened as they went deeper. Through the porthole, Max watched the rocks and seaweed flash by. He caught Lia's eye and they grinned at each other. Max could hardly contain his excitement. He knew Cora wouldn't be expecting them to go on the attack. This was their chance to beat her, and make Nemos safe from her threat once and for all.

She's going to get the shock of her life! Max thought to himself.

CHAPTER TWO

A NASTY SHOCK

The *Leaping Dolphin* raced through the water. Max sat in the co-pilot's seat, next to his mother. Ahead, shoals of silver fish flashed through the dark green water. He saw Spike swimming beside them. Max sensed how nimbly the sub responded as his mother steered, and the engine note was throaty and powerful. The *Leaping Dolphin* was in tip-top condition, there was no doubt about that.

Max had already powered up the sub's

blaster cannon. He'd come up with a plan and explained it to the others as they'd travelled towards Cora. It was risky, perhaps – but Max felt confident it would work.

He glanced at the radar screen. To his surprise he saw two pulsing yellow blobs moving towards the central dot that was the *Leaping Dolphin*. He could tell from the shape that one was Cora on the aquabike. The other one was beside her, and not much bigger.

"She's got something with her!" he said.

"A Robobeast?" his mother said.

"Must be a fairly small one, if so," Max said. "Nothing to worry about." But even as he said it, he felt a prickle of nerves.

"There she is!" shouted Lia.

Max looked through the viewing screen again. His heart leaped as he saw Cora, underwater now, sitting astride the aquabike

– *his* aquabike – with her long black hair flowing out behind her. She wore the silver Robobeast-control device on her head and an Amphibio mask on her face. And next to her was one of the oddest-looking Robobeasts Max had ever seen.

It was a sort of fish, of a funny shape, and it looked somehow baggy and loose, like a deflated balloon. It was a murky yellow

colour, and had big, round, dark eyes. There was a metal tube attached to its back, and two metal barrels strapped to its sides. The attachments looked almost too heavy for it to manage. It wore an oversized metal collar with a name engraved on a badge at the front: GUBBIX.

Is this some kind of joke? Max wondered. Gubbix didn't seem the least bit dangerous. It looked almost comical. Max felt glad that, if his plan worked, they would be able to control the creature without having to fight it. He would have felt guilty attacking this baggy, feeble-looking creature. Why had Cora even brought it along? *She probably reckoned she would have already beaten us by now, with one of the other, stronger Robobeasts,* Max thought. *But she didn't, and now this funny-looking thing is all she's got left!*

Niobe slewed the sub to a halt directly

in front of Cora, who stopped too. Max moved the blaster controls so that one of the cannons was aimed at the strange fish and the other at Cora.

Cora didn't seem worried. She touched her headpiece and it slid down over the top half of her face like a visor, with the microphone positioned in front of her Amphibio mask.

"How nice of you to come and meet me to surrender!" Her voice echoed through the sub's aqua-sound speakers. "It's saved me the bother of chasing you."

"Sandwiches," Rivet growled, as menacingly as he could.

Max spoke into the Communication Panel on the console. "We're not here to surrender, Cora. We're here for a showdown."

"A showdown!" Cora smirked. "How dramatic. And how brave of you! Stupid, obviously, but brave."

Max bit back a sharp retort. *Don't let her get to you. We hold the upper hand.* "Listen, we'll offer you a deal. Give yourself up and join the Professor in jail. Then we don't have to destroy you – or the Robobeast."

Cora chuckled. "I like the idea of a deal, but you haven't got the terms quite right. I know you've been making a compass to guide yourselves out of the Lost Lagoon. So how about this: you give me that compass, as well as the gem. It's made of Mentlium, in case you were wondering. That's the same material your foolish uncle used on Skalda the Soul Stealer. Mentlium has the power to control minds, which is why I need it back. So give me the gem and the compass, and in return I won't kill you. That's pretty generous, isn't it? You can stay here in the Lost Lagoon, all nice and safe, while I get on with taking over the whole of Nemos."

"Sorry, you're not tempting us, Cora!" Max said. "I guess we'll have to settle this the old-fashioned way."

He looked at his mother. She nodded, and slipped out of the pilot's seat. Max slid into her place. Lia was already making her way to the exit hatch. Max gave her a thumbs-up sign. There was no need for words; everyone knew what to do.

A moment later, Lia and Niobe swam out in front of the *Leaping Dolphin* and stopped in front of Cora and Gubbix, treading water. Spike was beside them, his swordlike bill pointing at the enemy. Max felt a bit guilty – he didn't like sitting here in safety while his mother and Lia faced Cora. But it was all part of the plan.

He spoke into the Comms panel. "Mum – use the Mentlium!"

Niobe clutched the gem that was pinned

to her tunic, and her eyes flashed green. She stared at Cora Blackheart and then at the Robobeast and spoke in a slow and commanding voice. "Do as I say: drop all your weapons, and give yourself up."

Max saw a flicker in Gubbix's eyes, as though they had momentarily turned green. But apart from that, it didn't respond.

Cora just laughed. "Did you really think I wouldn't have a way to resist the Mentlium's power? Just because you're stupid, that doesn't mean everyone else is! Gubbix is immune to the Mentlium. And as for me, the control visor protects me!"

An icy hand seemed to grip Max's heart. He had sent his mum and Lia out into danger! They were floating helplessly in the water in front of a Robobeast and the deadliest pirate on Nemos.

"Gubbix," said Cora. "Prepare to attack!"

Max watched in disbelief as the Robobeast began to grow.

And grow.

And grow.

The metal tube on its head straightened

out and pointed at Niobe. The end of the tube glowed reddish-orange, as if getting ready to erupt. The barrels along its sides suddenly fired up, with tongues of flame shooting out behind. And sharp spikes, like swords, bristled out from its rubbery skin.

It's some sort of pufferfish, Max thought, remembering the friendly one Lia had shown him once, not far from Sumara. But Gubbix looked far less friendly. It was at least three times as big as the sub – one of the biggest Robobeasts they had ever faced. His mind raced helplessly. *There must be something I can do*, he thought. *But what?*

"Isn't he lovely?" Cora said. "Those barbs contain lethal venom. I bet you wish you'd accepted my terms now, don't you? But you didn't, so I'm afraid...you die."

"Quick! Mum! Lia! Get back in the sub now!" Max shouted.

But before either Max's mum or Lia
could move, two of the barbs shot out
from Gubbix's hide, straight towards them,
zooming through the water like a pair of
poisoned arrows.

CHAPTER THREE

POISONED BARBS

Max was so horrified that everything seemed to happen in slow motion. The poison darts streaked towards Niobe and Lia. With a flip of her finlike feet, Lia dodged the barb. But his mum wasn't so quick.

WHOOSH-THUMP!

Max saw a large, silvery shape crash into his mother and send her flying clear of the dart's path. It took him a moment to make sense of what had happened – Spike had swum to his mum's rescue, knocking her out of the way!

"Back to the sub!" Max shouted. He manoeuvred the craft closer to Niobe and Lia. At the same time, he trained both blaster cannons on Gubbix. *I'll give that Robobeast something to think about!* he thought, pressing the firing button.

The twin missiles powered through the water. In a flash, Gubbix deflated, shrinking back to a third of its size. The missiles passed harmlessly over its head.

But at least Max had distracted the monster from attacking his mum and Lia again. He heard the entrance hatch open above him and then the airlock door, and breathed out in relief as Niobe and Lia came scrambling down into the sub.

"Great plan, Max!" Lia said sarcastically. "Got any more?"

"Yes, actually," Max said. "Let's get out of here!"

"Good thinking," Max's mother said. "That thing is too powerful if we can't use the brooch on it."

Max spun the wheel to turn the sub around.

"Where do you think you're going?" came Cora's voice. "We haven't finished playing yet!"

We've got to fight back, Max thought. "Take the wheel, Mum," he said. "You get us out of here. I'll try to keep Cora busy."

The *Leaping Dolphin* surged away, but Cora and the Robobeast came after them.

"Come on, Spike," yelled Lia, watching her swordfish dart ahead of them and out of harm's way.

Max tapped quickly on the sub's weapons panel, firing up the rear blaster cannons. With one hand he gripped the joystick control. He picked out Cora's shape on the camera feed and aimed at the aquabike. It would be a pity to destroy his bike, but if he could blast it out from under her—

"Look out!" shouted Lia.

Max turned and saw, through the viewing screen, the two barbs that Gubbix had fired turn and come shooting back through the green water towards them. Their tips flashed

red. *Oh no!* Max thought. *They're heat-seeking darts!*

Max's mother spun the wheel frantically.

THUNKKK-THUNKKK!

The two darts hit the side of the sub simultaneously. The *Leaping Dolphin* rocked crazily. Max had to cling to the side of his seat. Lia crashed into the wall and Rivet went somersaulting from one end of the sub to

the other, barking, "Sandwiches!"

Max saw with horror that the flashing red tips of the barbs were sticking right through the hull. Black poison dripped from them onto the floor. Worse, water was streaming in through the cracks the darts had made.

The *Leaping Dolphin*'s alarm system kicked into life. The warning lights on the console started flashing wildly, while an earsplitting robotic voice burst out: "ALERT! HULL BREACHED! ALERT! HULL BREACHED!"

"Stop that horrible noise!" said Lia with her hands over her ears.

Niobe punched a button on the console and the alarm stopped, but it was immediately replaced by Cora Blackheart's voice over the speaker.

"Gubbix, shall we give them some more?"

In the camera-feed, Max saw Gubbix swell monstrously and shoot a deadly hail of spikes. He braced himself—

THUNKKK-THUNKKK-THUNKKK-THUNKKK-THUNKKK-THUNKKK!

This time the impact was far worse. The sub shook violently, as if a giant hand had grabbed it. Max was hurled from his seat, along with his mother. Rolling helplessly on the floor, he saw more of the sword-like spikes jammed through the hull, dripping black poison. Water was spraying in through the holes with a deadly hiss. It was already ankle-deep.

"We're filling up!" Max's mum gasped.

"So what? We can all breathe underwater," Lia said.

"But the water will be filled with that deadly venom!" Max said, pointing at the dripping poison that was turning the water dark. It had already risen to the level of their knees. "We can't breathe that!"

"We have to get out!" Max's mother said.

She swayed towards the iron ladder that led to the airlock. But suddenly the sub stopped rocking. A strange red glow filled the interior of the *Leaping Dolphin*.

Max raced back to the pilot's seat. Through the viewing screen, he saw with dread the big shadowy eyes and bloated form of Gubbix. A

reddish-orange beam shone from the silver tube on its head, straight at the *Leaping Dolphin*. Gubbix began to swim backwards, and the *Leaping Dolphin* was pulled along with it.

"It's a tractor beam!" Max said. "It's hauling us along!"

"Aren't you a clever lad?" came Cora's mocking voice. "Always good to know what's going on, isn't it? Even if you can't do anything about it!"

Oh, can't I? thought Max. *We'll see about that!*

He yanked at the thruster lever. The *Leaping Dolphin*'s engine roared into life. Max could feel the sub judder as it tried to pull away from Gubbix's tractor beam. The engine note rose to a scream – but nothing happened. Gubbix continued to pull them along, its spooky face gazing in.

Cora appeared beside the Robobeast on the aquabike, grinning. "Ooh, you're taking on a lot of water there! I hope for your sake we get to where we're going before it reaches your noses!"

"Where are you taking us?" shouted Max.

"Wouldn't you like to know?" said Cora, and laughed.

The black water carried on rising around them, and they had to scramble up on their seats to escape it. The poison gave it a horrible, acidic stink.

"Sandwiches!" barked Rivet desperately.

"Don't worry, boy," Max said. "We've got out of tighter spots than this!"

I'm not sure that's really true, he thought.

"What's happened to Spike?" asked Lia. "I can't see him any more. Do you think he's following us?"

"Sure," Max said. "He's a smart fish, he'll

be keeping out of sight. He might be able to help us, if we – I mean *when* we get out of here."

The water was waist-deep now.

Let's hope it doesn't get to our mouths…

"I'm going to find out where they're taking us," Max's mum said. She waded to the console and pressed the touchpad for the *Leaping Dolphin*'s Mapping System. But the screen stayed blank.

"The computer systems are down!" Niobe said.

And then the lights went out.

The poisoned water was up to their chests now. Max's lungs ached with each breath. The fumes burned the back of his throat.

"We have to get out of here!" Max panted. His voice was hoarse and croaky.

He half-swam, half-waded towards the airlock. Niobe and Lia followed. Max clambered up the ladder. But as he began to open the escape hatch, there was a startling *CLANG!* and the door slammed shut, nearly trapping his fingers. Max fell back into the poisoned water with a splash. He realised immediately what had happened – Gubbix

must have knocked the escape hatch shut with one of its barbs.

"Did you think I'd let you out?" Cora's voice gloated over the aquaspeaker. "You're staying right there!"

Max looked at Lia and his mum. He could just make out their heads in the darkness. All of them were panting for breath, and the water had risen to their necks.

And it was still rising.

CHAPTER FOUR

MENTLIUM

"Hold your breath, everyone!" Max shouted.

He had to raise his head to speak – the poisoned water was almost touching his lips.

They all took a deep breath. Max could just make out the strained faces and the bulging eyes of the other two in the gloom. And Rivet, unaffected, of course.

Maybe this is it, Max thought. *The end of the line.* But how could he give up after they'd fought so hard?

There was a sudden jolt. The water sloshed up and down. But it stopped rising. Max felt the sub being lifted up. In the bit of the viewing screen that wasn't covered by the inky water, Max saw sky. Relief flooded through him. They weren't safe yet. But they weren't dead, either.

"Leave the submarine now!" Cora's voice commanded.

"You two go first," Max gasped. He'd got an idea. "Here, Riv!" he said quietly. The dogbot paddled over to him. Feeling beneath the water, Max opened Rivet's side panel and slipped his hyperblade inside.

"Sandwiches?" said Rivet.

"Just look after that," Max said. *Cora will take our weapons, but she won't think to look inside Rivet!* he thought.

Max followed his mum and Lia out through the hatch. He stood on the top of the sub with them, dripping and shivering.

Gubbix's tractor beam was holding the *Leaping Dolphin* in midair. In front of them was a high, vertical cliff-face of dark brown rock. Just above sea-level was a cave. Max saw his aquabike moored next to it.

So this is Cora's hideout, Max thought. She was standing on a rocky platform just inside, the silver visor over her eyes, holding a blaster in one hand and her electric cat-o-nine-tails in the other.

"You look like drowned rats," Cora said. "Put them down here, Gubbix."

The inflated pufferfish was bobbing on the surface of the water, like a buoy. It gradually lowered its tractor beam, and the *Leaping Dolphin* landed with a slight bump on the rocky platform in front of Cora. Max, his mum and Lia slid down from the top of the sub and faced her.

"Let's not waste time," Cora said. "Hand over the brooch and the compass!"

But Max's mum stood still, staring defiantly at Cora. Max felt a throb of pride at his mum's bravery.

There was a long pause.

"You can't have it!" shouted Lia.

Cora Blackheart smiled. "You prefer the hard way? Fine by me." She muttered something into the microphone attached to her visor.

A split second later, Max heard a swishing sound. Out of the corner of his eye, he saw something hurtling towards him, and threw himself flat.

One of Gubbix's venomous barbs whistled over his head. It hit the cliff wall with a *THUD*, and stuck there, quivering.

Cora grinned. "Nice reflexes. Reckon you could dodge ten at once?"

"All right, enough!" Max's mum said. "I'll give you what you want, just don't hurt Max."

"No, Mum!" Max shouted – but his mother was already moving towards Cora, unpinning the brooch from her tunic.

"Thank you!" Cora said, tucking her blaster under her arm as she took the brooch. "It's just what I wanted!" Her eyes turned green as she stared at Niobe. Max's heart sank as he saw his mother's face go blank. She was under the spell of the Mentlium. "Now," said Cora, "what about that compass? How do I make it work?"

"It's not complete," Niobe answered, in a flat, monotonous voice. "It has to have a needle of Barrum."

"Is that right?" Cora said. "And where can I find some Barrum?"

"Don't tell her, Mum!" Max shouted, though he knew it was hopeless.

"In the Underwater Market," Niobe said. "It's not far from here—"

"I know where it is," Cora interrupted, grinning victoriously. "So all I need is the compass itself. Where is it?"

"In Max's pocket," said Niobe in a dull voice. Max knew his mother couldn't help answering, but still he despaired.

"Let's have it then, boy!" said Cora. She gripped the brooch, shifting her gaze to Max. He quickly covered his face with his hands before Cora could catch his eye.

Yes! That seemed to work – he felt no urge to obey. *You must need direct eye contact for the Mentlium to take effect*, Max thought. *If only I'd known that in time to warn Mum!*

"Enough messing about!" Cora said in a knife-sharp voice. "Give me the compass!"

Max still refused to look at her. Peeping through a chink in his fingers, to the side of him, he saw that Lia had followed his lead and covered her eyes, too. Good – that was two of them, plus Rivet, who weren't affected. Maybe they still had a chance...

"You're only prolonging the agony!" Cora

said. "But if that's the way you want it…
Gubbix!"

Max cringed, knowing the Robobeast
would be shooting its poisonous barbs at
them. He felt vulnerable, not able to see the
attack. A moment later he heard the darts
whistle through the air and shouted to Lia,
"Dodge!"

Listening as hard as he could, he hurled
himself to one side as the poisoned darts flew
past. As he rolled he saw that Lia, too, had
also managed to dive out of the way. Then he
hastily covered his eyes again, in case Cora
managed to lock gazes with him.

Max heard footsteps, and was aware of a
shadow falling over him where he lay. *Cora.*

He heard Rivet barking "Sandwiches!"

"You can't have the compass!" Max
shouted. "And I won't look at you!"

"Don't worry, Max," said a soft, gentle

voice. "This will be quick."

A chill ran through Max. The voice was his mother's.

He looked up and saw her standing over him, her eyes blank, her face a mask. She was

holding a large, jagged grey rock in her right hand.

"Mum!" shouted Max. "Stop! You have to fight it!"

"Don't be stupid, Max," Cora said. "No one can fight Mentlium. Niobe – kill Max! Lia – you kill him too!"

Max scrambled to his feet. With a shock he saw that Lia was under the spell – she must have accidentally glanced at Cora. She was also holding a rock, and her face was as blank as his mother's.

Max backed away. His mother and Lia advanced, staring dully.

He reached the back wall of the cave, the spiky rock digging into his back. There was nowhere to run.

"Go on," said Cora. "Smash his brains out!"

His mother and Lia raised their rocks, ready to strike.

Max raised his hands to ward off the blows. But how could he defend himself against both of them at once?

CHAPTER FIVE

UNDERWATER MARKET

"Sandwiches!" barked Rivet.

Max turned his head to see the dogbot take a heroic leap into the air, smashing into Cora with the full weight of his chunky metal body.

Cora was knocked off her feet and fell flat on her back. The impact knocked the Mentlium brooch from her hand. She screamed in rage. "No!"

"Max!" said Niobe. Her eyes had returned

to normal. She looked at the rock she was holding and shuddered, letting it fall to the ground. Lia dropped hers too.

"I'm so sorry, Max, I nearly—" said his mother.

"It's not your fault, Mum. Quick, we have to get out of here!"

Cora was on her hands and knees now, scrabbling around for the brooch, which had fallen somewhere on the rocky ground.

Max, Niobe and Lia ran to the cave mouth.

"Stop them, Gubbix!" Cora shouted as they ran past.

Max flinched, instinctively. Then he saw that Gubbix wasn't there any more.

"Look!" shouted Lia. Far out to sea, Max saw the giant pufferfish chasing a silvery shape that kept leaping out of the water. "It's Spike," Lia said. "He's distracted Gubbix."

"Now's our chance to escape!" Max looked

at the *Leaping Dolphin*. It lay on the rock like a wounded animal, the metal barbs sticking out from its punctured hull. *We won't be going anywhere in that...* Then his eyes landed on the aquabike, the one that Cora had stolen from him, moored and bobbing in the sea.He leaped eagerly onto it. "Climb aboard, everyone!"

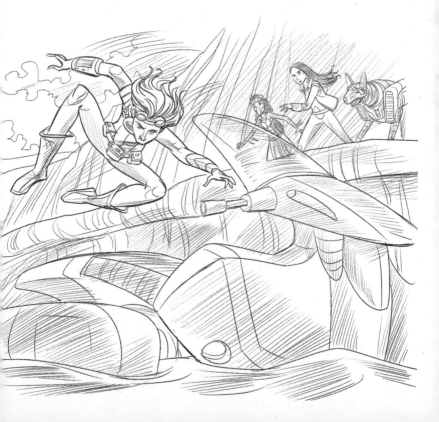

His mum, Lia and Rivet piled on behind him as Max revved the throttle.

"Sandwiches!" growled Rivet. Max glanced back and saw that Cora had risen to her feet. She didn't have the brooch yet but she raised her blaster, her face twisting with rage.

Max tilted the handlebars down. The aquabike dived beneath the water just as the first blaster-shot passed overhead.

"Next stop, the Underwater Market!" Max said.

Lia pulled her Amphibio mask off as Spike came swimming up beside them. The super-fast swordfish had no trouble keeping up with the aquabike. "You genius!" Lia said. She pushed off from the aquabike and landed on Spike's back, patting his head. "We'd never have got past Gubbix without you."

"Cora must have called the Robobeast back," Niobe said. "She'll use it to come after us – she knows where we're going, remember. I'm so sorry I told her!"

"It wasn't your fault, Mum," Max said. "Don't worry, we'll reach the Underwater Market first. We'll get the Barrum, and be out of there before she can find us!"

"We should surface, then," Max's mother said. "Visibility's better up there – we'll be able to spot the pillars in the distance."

"Do we have to?" Lia complained. "I've just got used to breathing water again!"

"You and Spike can stay below," Max said. "But close to the surface – keep us in sight."

He tilted the handlebars upwards and the bike began to rise. Moments later, the aquabike leaped out of the water and landed with a bump, spraying foam around. Rivet leaped off the bike, and paddled alongside them. It was a sunny day, and in the distance, Max saw the four great pillars of the Underwater Market sticking up from the glittering blue ocean.

"There it is!" he shouted.

"We've really put one over on Cora this time!" his mother said.

As long as it doesn't take too long to find the Barrum, Max thought. He made the aquabike dive again, and they rejoined Lia and Spike, streaking towards the market.

The Underwater Market was big. In fact, it was huge. As they drew near, Max saw that between the rocky pillars there were multiple levels of stone floors, and every floor was crammed with stalls and traders. It was so crowded that there wasn't room for everyone, and some customers were swimming around on the edges, just outside the pillars.

Max saw all kinds of creatures he didn't

recognise, some with horns and fins, some with tentacles, and even one strange being that looked like a man but had big red claws like a lobster's. These were clearly inhabitants of the Lost Lagoon – at least, he had never seen anything like them in the rest of Nemos. But there were also humanoid people who looked Merryn, or Aquoran – possibly travellers who had found their way into the Lost Lagoon and never been able to get out again. Music was playing, a loud, swirling tune that reminded Max of fairground music back on Aquora.

It's going to be difficult to find the Barrum in all that chaos, he thought.

"We need to split up," Max said. "It'll be quicker. Lia and Spike, you search the bottom floors. Mum, you take the middle. Rivet and If will cover the top floors, won't we, boy?"

"Sandwiches!" came the inevitable reply.

"We can stay in touch via our headsets," said Niobe. "As soon as anyone finds the Barrum, let the others know – we have to get out of here before Cora arrives with Gubbix!"

Lia and Spike dived down towards the lowest floor. Max's mum kicked off from the aquabike, swam to the middle level and was soon lost in the crowds.

Max took the bike up to the top level. There was a docking station on one side of it, with bays where craft could be tied up. There were plenty of interesting-looking submersibles there, some pretty hi-tech, and Max would have liked to stop and take a look. But there was no time to spare – Cora would be coming after them with perhaps the deadliest Robobeast they had ever faced, and the Mentlium gem.

Max parked the aquabike at the docking station in a hurry and pushed his way into the market, with Rivet at his heels.

It was noisy in the market. Competing with the music was the sound of traders and customers haggling in a hundred different languages. Max passed a stall selling weapons, where two Colossids – the giant spiders they had met on the Island of Illusion – were examining battle-axes, talking in their strange, clicking speech.

"Do you know where I could find some Barrum?" he asked.

The Colossids ignored him. The stallholder, who looked like a clam on legs, said in halting Merryn: "No, no Barrum. Barrum not good for weapons."

Max moved on. He passed stalls selling a bewildering variety of food, coral artwork, musical instruments and maps, as well as clothing, lamps and weird, oddly-shaped objects whose purpose he couldn't even guess.

But no Barrum. He asked every stallholder he met, and they all shook their heads, or shrugged, or waved their fins vaguely.

Max felt increasingly desperate. Cora knew where to look for them, and she couldn't be far away now...

He flicked his headset on and asked his mother if she had had any luck.

"Not yet, Max. But I'm looking."

He tried Lia next. "Anything?"

"No Barrum, but I did buy some Dock Kelp. They said it was an antidote to blowfish venom – it could come in handy if Gubbix catches up with us!"

"Yes," said Max. "But let's hurry up and find the Barrum, then we can be out of here before Gubbix arrives."

He turned to Rivet. "This is getting desperate. I think we should start shouting out what we're looking for."

"Sandwiches!" barked Rivet. "Sandwiches!"

A trader who looked like a giant fish beckoned them to his stall. "You want food, my friends? I have seaweed fritters, prawn rolls, kelp-cakes..."

Max groaned. "You'd better leave this to

me," he told Rivet. Then he shouted as loud as he could, "Barrum! Barrum! Has anyone here got any Barrum?"

"You want Barrum?" A tentacle tugged at Max's arm, and he turned to see a figure in a long black cloak with the astonished black eyes and beaked face of a squid. "You've come to the right place."

He pulled Max towards a stall which was hung with strips and sheets of metal, some gold, some silver, and others shimmering with rainbow hues. "I am Sellius, dealer in rare and precious metals," said the squid-person in Aquoran, gesturing with more tentacles that appeared from beneath his cloak.

"Please, this is urgent," Max said. He held out his hand and Sellius shook it with the end of a tentacle. "Do you have Barrum?"

"Of course I have Barrum! I also have

white gold, platinum, zinc, copper..."

Max shook his head. "No, all I need is the Barrum – and fast!"

"No problem, my friend. How will you be paying for that?"

"Er—" For the first time, Max realised that this might be an issue. "I haven't actually got any money, as such..."

Sellius's beak dropped open. "No money? He comes to a market with no money? Well, have you anything to trade?"

"Not really, I don't—"

"So I'm supposed to give my precious metals away, is that it?" said Sellius. "Don't they have markets where you come from?"

"Wait, let me think..." It was agonising to be so close to the last metal and not be able to buy it – and Cora was getting nearer with every heartbeat.

"And now he wants to think!" Sellius said. "You should have thought before you came to the market, my friend!"

Suddenly an idea came to Max. "Here, Rivet!" he said. The dogbot trotted over. Max bent to open the side panel. He didn't want to lose his hyperblade, but he had nothing else to trade.

"Oh, you have a robot pet," Sellius said. "They're good, aren't they? I have one too." He produced a shrill whistling sound, and from behind the stall a silvery robotic crab slowly sidled out. Max noticed that one claw was much bigger than the other.

"Pinch, he's called. He's my metal-cutter!" Sellius said. "Or he was, but his claw doesn't work so well now. Pinch can't pinch. Something's wrong with him, but I don't know how to fix it. What am I, a mechanic?"

"I know a bit about robotics!" Max said, eagerly. "If I fixed him – would you give me some Barrum?"

Sellius waved his tentacles around enthusiastically. "You fix him well enough to cut you some Barrum, and he'll cut you some Barrum! We have a deal!"

Max kneeled and turned Pinch onto its back. Its legs waved around feebly. "Don't worry, I won't hurt you," Max said. He flipped open the control panel. Inside was a silver battery and a mass of tangled wires. In a moment, Max saw what was wrong. The wires weren't properly connected. Not a complicated job to fix it – but a fiddly one.

"Max! Max!" His mother's voice rang out to him. He looked round and saw her and Lia riding towards him on Spike.

"Hi, Mum!" Max grinned. "If I just fix this little robot, we get the Barrum!"

"But there's no time!" Lia shouted. Her face was tight with worry. "Cora and Gubbix are already here!"

CHAPTER SIX

SINGLE COMBAT

Max felt a burning sense of frustration. He was so close to getting the Barrum! "I just need a bit more time!" he said.

"We don't have more time," his mother said. "She's here now, at the market!"

"But she hasn't found us yet," Max said. He bent and tried to concentrate on the task. The wires were small and kept slipping through his fingers.

"Hurry up!" Lia said.

"I am hurrying up!"

Max heard screams. Gubbix must be very close now. But *he* was very close too...

He put the last wire in place and snapped the panel shut.

Pinch's claw opened and shut with a satisfying snap. The robocrab flipped over onto its legs and ran round and round, clicking its claws.

"Nice job!" said Sellius. He pulled down a strip of gleaming red metal from the back of the stall. "A deal is a deal – how much you do want?"

"Just a little – no bigger than a needle!" said Max's mum. "But be quick!"

The screaming was getting louder. People swam past them, looking frightened, although Gubbix wasn't in view yet.

"What's all that noise?" Sellius said, looking around. "What's going on?"

"Please," said Max. "You have to hurry, just

give us the Barrum!"

"All right, all right... Pinch – cut me a tiny strip of this, will you?" Sellius passed the sheet of metal to the robocrab. Pinch snipped off a needle-sized sliver and presented it to Max.

People were rushing past, swimming as fast as they could, barging into one another in their haste to get away.

Max handed the Barrum, with the compass,

to his mother. Speedily, she fitted the needle into place. Max shoved the device back in his pocket.

"We've done it!" Max said. "Now let's—"

A huge shadow fell over him. He looked up, and saw the giant, balloon-like shape of Gubbix floating above. Cora was right by its side, holding her blaster.

"Don't look at her!" Max's mother said. "The Mentlium!"

Max gazed down at the stone floor. He knew he had to think fast. They had the compass now. If they could reach the aquabike before Cora could get them...

"Listen to me, everyone," came Cora's voice. "Look up at me, that's right. Now stay where you are."

The screaming stopped. All the traders and customers stood stock still.

"You see those three outsiders there, with

the robodog, by the precious-metals stall? You don't let them out of here, do you hear?"

The market-goers advanced, forming a circle around them. A ring of faces stared at Max and his friends. The faces belonged to many kinds of creature, but they shared the same empty expression, and all were eerily silent. They were under Cora's spell. No chance of getting past them to reach the aquabike now.

"It looks like I'm just in time to pick up the compass," said Cora. "Let's have it!"

Max, Niobe and Lia continued to look down, not meeting Cora's eyes.

"All right, let me make this as simple as I possibly can!" the pirate said. "Max, bring me the compass right now – or I'll make Gubbix shoot a poisoned dart at your mother and your sweet little friend Lia. They'll die a slow, painful death, all because of your stubbornness. You wouldn't want that on your conscience, would you?"

Max could have cried with rage. *How can we be beaten at the last gasp, when we're so close to success?* Suddenly, he had an idea. It wouldn't give them much of a chance, but it was all he had.

"You're very brave when you're protected by a Robobeast, aren't you?" he shouted to Cora. "And when you've got the Mentlium brooch. I bet you wouldn't be so brave if you didn't have them!"

"I know what you're trying to do," Cora said. "And it won't work! Bring me the compass!"

"I don't blame you, though. Last time we fought, on the Island of Illusion, one on one, I beat you. You ran away, didn't you, Cora?"

"No I didn't!" Cora said. Max heard anger in her voice, and it gave him a thrill of hope.

"You did, Cora. You're just a coward really, aren't you?" said Niobe, joining in. "You call yourself 'Captain Blackheart', and you're afraid to fight a boy!"

"A lot of people are watching, Cora," Max said. "Hundreds of people. This won't do your reputation much good. They'll remember when they come out of their trance. She was scared of a boy, that's what they'll say. It will spread all over the Lost Lagoon – probably all over Nemos, eventually!"

"This is great, Max!" whispered Lia.

There was a long pause. Max could hear his own heart beating.

"All right!" Cora snapped at last. "Since you're so desperate to die, I'll oblige!"

"A fair fight?" Max said. "One on one? No brooch?"

"No brooch!" Cora said. "I've hung it on one of Gubbix's spines. Now you'll get what's coming to you!"

"Be careful, Max!" said his mum. She squeezed his hand.

Max looked up. The brooch dangled from one of Gubbix's barbs. Cora held two more of the barbs, one in each hand.

"But you haven't got a weapon, Max!" Lia said.

"Haven't I?" Max said. He opened Rivet's side panel and took out the hyperblade.

"Prepare to die, Max!" Cora shouted. She swam down and landed in the circle made by the crowd of market-goers and traders. Sellius was watching, as glassy-eyed as the rest of them.

Max faced Cora squarely. At least she wouldn't be able to use her cat-o-nine-tails under water, that was one blessing. But those barbs looked deadly.

"Let's just establish the rules—" Cora

began, but before she even finished her
sentence, she threw one of the barbs at Max.
It streaked through the water like a torpedo.
He dived to one side, but not fast enough:
the spike tore into his shoulder.

"No!" yelled Niobe and Lia together.

Immediately Max could feel the black poison seeping into the wound. It stung like acid.

"Got you!" said Cora. "Now, let's finish you off in the traditional style!"

She lunged at Max with the other barb.

Max parried with his hyperblade, knocking the blow aside. Cora might be taller and stronger, but he was faster. Her guard was momentarily down, and Max attacked, swiping, slicing, making her give up ground. The crowd behind her parted as she was forced backwards.

But Max could feel his strength draining. The poison was in his bloodstream now, making him sluggish and confused. How much longer could he keep this up?

Cora recovered her balance and thrust at him once more with the barb. Max parried again. But the poison's effects were getting worse and worse. The market seemed to spin around him, and he sank to his knees.

Cora smiled at Max. "I'd better put you out of your misery, hadn't I?"

She pointed the barb directly at his heart and lunged.

Reacting instinctively, Max beat the blow back. But the effort was too much. He felt the last of his strength ebb away. The hyperblade was knocked from his hand and drifted down to the stone floor, and he didn't have the energy to grab for it. He could barely stay upright.

Cora hooked her leg behind his and pushed. Max fell on his back.

Captain Blackheart stood over him and raised the metal barb.

CHAPTER SEVEN

A COMMAND PERFORMANCE

"Fun's over," Cora said. "Goodbye, Max." Then she paused. "Wait a minute. I asked you to do something and you didn't do it. And you know, I do like to be obeyed. Gubbix!"

The great pufferfish swam over to her. She took the Mentlium brooch from its spine and put it on. Her eyes flashed green.

"No!" shouted Niobe. Lying on the ground, Max was aware of a commotion as the crowd held his mother and Lia back, preventing them intervening.

"Look me in the eyes, Max!"

Cora Blackheart stooped over him. Max knew he should look away. But the poison had dulled his reactions. Before he could turn his head or shut his eyes, Cora's eyes locked onto his.

"Now give me the compass, Max," she said softly.

Max lay still. In a moment, he guessed, the Mentlium would overcome him. But... nothing happened. He felt no urge to obey Cora's command. *Strange*, he thought. *Why isn't it working?*

And then he had a flash of inspiration. *Gubbix is immune to the Mentlium's power*, he remembered. *And I've got Gubbix's venom in my bloodstream now. Maybe – maybe that means I'm immune too?*

That gave him a small advantage. Cora wouldn't be expecting any resistance from him now.

He got slowly to his feet, pretending to be under the Mentlium spell, and fumbled in his pocket.

"That's a good lad," Cora said, holding out her hand.

Max got right up close to her. He pulled out the compass. And as she took it from his hand, he leaned forward and snatched the brooch from her tunic.

"What? You little—"

She sliced at him with her spike, but he had already staggered back out of range. He pushed his way into the crowd.

"Stop him!" shouted Cora.

But the market-goers were coming out their trance now that Cora no longer had the brooch. They were muttering angrily among themselves and shooting evil looks at the pirate.

Max rushed back to Sellius's stall and to Pinch, the robot crab. He put the Mentlium gem in the crab's claw. "Crush it, Pinch! Break it to pieces!"

The robocrab's powerful pincers closed. There was a grinding, cracking sound. Then the gem exploded into a shower of green fragments and dust.

"Noooo!" shouted Cora.

She began to stride towards Max.

"No you don't!" shouted Niobe. She ran in front of Cora, and so did Lia – and then the crowd seemed suddenly to come to life. Waving hands and fins and tentacles, they surged towards Cora and surrounded her.

Max was feeling seriously groggy now. The words of the crowd came to him as if from a great distance.

"What shall we do with her?" said Sellius.

"Put her in prison!"

"Feed her to the sharks!"

"Gubbix!" shrieked Cora. "Tractor beam!"

The giant pufferfish's tractor beam suddenly shone out, catching Cora in its red glow.

"Away, Gubbix!" Cora shouted.

The Robobeast's rocket blasters powered up and it swam away, dragging Cora along in its tractor beam. They zoomed over the heads

of the crowd and away.

"She's gone!" Lia said. "And she's got the compass! We can't stop her getting out of the Lost Lagoon now!"

Her words sounded weird and distorted to Max. He took a step towards her, tottered, and fell.

"Max!" he heard his mother cry.

Then she was cradling his head on her knees.

The poison...it's really kicking in, Max thought. *At least I died trying to do good, trying to defeat evil. Mum and Lia will have to take over now.*

He saw his mother's and Lia's faces above, but they were blurred and remote. He felt himself slipping away. *So this is what dying feels like*, he thought.

Everything went black.

CHAPTER EIGHT

ATTACK OF THE TURTLES

Then Max felt a touch on his shoulder. A warm feeling spread through him, soothing away the pain. *Dying isn't so bad,* he thought. *No more pain.*

But he didn't feel as if he were dying. Instead his whole body was tingling with energy. He opened his eyes.

Lia and his mum were still bent over him. Lia was tucking some green stuff in the pocket of her tunic. Rivet thrust his metal nose in Max's face.

"Thank Vorn you're all right!" said Max's mother.

Max sat up. "What happened?"

"The Dock Kelp," Lia said. "I told you it might come in handy! And it really works."

"I guess so! I feel back to normal," Max said. He stood up. "So where's Cora?"

Niobe's face fell. "She's on her way out of the Lagoon – we'll never catch her now." She pointed out into the green water. Far away, two orange lights were dimly visible – Gubbix's blaster rockets.

"Oh, we'll catch her," Max said. "We have the aquabike, remember! Let's go!"

"Sandwiches!" said Rivet once more, leading the way.

The crowd parted to let them through. Max caught sight of Sellius and Pinch, and waved. "Thanks!"

"Thank you," said Sellius, patting Pinch's shiny head. "And good luck!"

They swam to where Max had moored the aquabike. He jumped into the driver's seat, and his mother and Rivet climbed on behind. Lia sat astride Spike. The swordfish shot ahead, but Max twisted the throttle and roared after them, soon catching up.

The glow of Gubbix's blaster rockets grew bigger and brighter.

"We're gaining on them!" said Niobe.

Max gave the throttle an extra twist. The engine note rose, making the whole aquabike throb as it went even faster.

Gubbix's shape was large and definite ahead of them, with Cora sitting astride it.

She doesn't know we're after her, Max thought. *What a shock she'll get!*

"I think my Aqua Powers are back!" Lia

said suddenly. "There are rock turtles nearby, and I can feel their thoughts!"

"It must be because the brooch is destroyed," Niobe said. "I think its power has been interfering with everything natural here in the Lagoon."

"Hey, Spike! I can talk to you again!" Lia leaned forward, listening, then chuckled. "He says, 'About time!'"

They passed the rock turtles, a crowd of

big green creatures paddling swiftly along. But Max hardly looked at them; he only had eyes for Cora and Gubbix. He hunched low over the handlebars, bending his head to cut down on water resistance.

At that moment Cora looked round. She must have heard the aquabike's engine. Her eyes narrowed in a scowl.

Didn't expect us, did you? Max thought.

"Look," Niobe said. "That shimmering patch ahead – that must be the way out of the Lagoon!"

The water shifted and swirled and sparkled, in a colour he had never seen before.

How can that be? Max thought. *A colour I didn't even know existed!*

They were close to Gubbix now.

We have to watch out for those spikes, Max thought. "Let's go under him!" he said to Lia.

He dived beneath the pufferfish's huge

belly, with Lia on Spike beside him, and slewed the bike round to face Cora. "Going somewhere?" he said.

Cora's face was twisted with fury. "How many times do I have to beat you?" she asked.

"I could ask you the same," Max said with a grin.

Cora glared at him. "This will be the last time, I can promise you that!"

Max turned to Rivet. "Go on ahead, boy!" he said. "Send out a distress signal to the Aquoran fleet – Cora could be coming through at any moment."

"Gubbix!" Cora yelled.

The Robobeast inflated a little more, its spikes bristling dangerously.

Max turned to Lia and spoke in a low voice. "Those barbs are heat-seeking, right? Get ready to dodge – and then do what I do!"

Suddenly, five venomous darts shot out

from Gubbix's head, straight at them.

Max's reflexes kicked in. He swerved the bike violently downwards and to one side. Out of the corner of his eye he saw Lia veer off to the other side. The barbs shot harmlessly between them.

But they'd be coming back, Max knew.

"Hold on tight, Mum!" He steered the aquabike towards Gubbix, revved up, and charged straight at the Robobeast. Lia and Spike joined him, swimming straight towards the pufferfish. Max saw Cora's eyes go wide with alarm.

He heard the poisoned barbs swishing behind them, returning to seek them out.

"Now!" he said to Lia, and wrenched the handlebars. The aquabike peeled off to one side, and Spike peeled off to the other.

And the five heat-seeking barbs crashed straight into Gubbix's rocket blasters. The

blasters exploded into pieces and tumbled towards the ocean bed. Gubbix immediately began to deflate in shock. Cora almost fell off, but managed to keep her balance.

"You've annoyed me long enough!" Cora

said. "Gubbix – the tractor beam!"

The tube on the Robobeast's head was undamaged. The orange beam shone out and held the aquabike, and Spike, in its grip. Max revved and twisted the handlebars. The engine roared, but the bike didn't move.

"Finally I have you exactly where I want you!" Cora said. Her scowl was replaced with a horrible smile. "Let's pull you in a bit – so that I can't miss!" She raised her blaster pistol. The tractor beam pulled them closer to Gubbix.

Max glanced across at Lia. She had closed her eyes and was pressing her hands to her head.

The Aqua Powers, Max thought. *She's calling for help.* And then, in the distance, he saw a crowd of dark shapes, swiftly paddling towards them.

Cora aimed the blaster at Max's head.

"No!" said Max's mum.

"Yes," Cora said. "Now it's finally time to say goodbye."

The dark shapes behind Cora were getting bigger.

If I can just delay her for a few seconds, Max thought. *Buy a little bit of time...*

"You couldn't beat me in hand-to-hand combat – so you shoot me instead!" Max said. "Very brave!"

"What do you mean? I won!"

Max shrugged. "If that's what you call winning."

Cora gave a short, angry laugh. "You're not going to pull the same trick on me twice!"

The rock turtles were close behind now.

"You can't murder us in cold blood!" shouted Niobe.

"Just watch me." Cora's finger tightened on the trigger.

WHAMMM!

The crowd of big green rock turtles crashed into the deflating Gubbix.

Cora's blaster went off, but fired harmlessly upwards. The Robobeast's tractor beam switched off, and the aquabike lunged forward. Max jammed his foot on the brake.

Cora was knocked off the Robobeast and went spiralling down through the water. As she fell, Max saw the compass fall from her pocket, and quickly drove the aquabike over to scoop it up.

Lia's hands were still pressed to her head, Max saw. She was guiding the turtles, telling them what to do. A group of them butted the

tractor-beam tube on Gubbix's head until it came loose and floated away. Meanwhile, another turtle snatched the control device from Cora, and crunched it up in its beak.

Gubbix gave itself a shake and the metal spikes fell away. It was free, Max realised. No longer a Robobeast, but a natural creature of the ocean. It turned and began to swim

towards the evil pirate who had enslaved it.

"Gubbix! I always treated you well, didn't I?" Cora said.

The pufferfish moved towards her, rotating its fins, inflating menacingly.

Cora turned tail and swam away as fast as she could. The pufferfish darted after her, snapping at her heels.

Max watched them getting smaller as they disappeared back into the Lagoon.

"Do you think she'll get away?" Max said.

"My money would be on the fish," Niobe said. "But hopefully we'll never find out."

Lia patted the shell of one of the rock turtles. "Thanks, friends – you really helped us out there!" Then she stroked Spike's flank. "It's all right, you're still my best friend, no need to get jealous!"

"Let's get back to Nemos," Max said. He turned the aquabike. "I've got the compass.

Hang on, Mum."

He twisted the throttle and darted forward into the strange, shimmering patch of water.

CHAPTER NINE

SANDWICHES

Max was spun violently, round and round and up and down, the rainbow-coloured water shining all around him. It was as if they'd entered a giant whirlpool. He saw Lia and Spike nearby, whirling about, their eyes as wide as each other's. Behind him, he heard his mother gasp in awe and astonishment.

They popped out the other side into still, green waters, and somehow Max knew that they were back in Nemos.

"Oh, that feels so good!" Lia said. "Home again!"

In front of them, Max saw a line of Aquoran vessels, ready in the water as if waiting for them. Beyond, he could see the black shapes of battleship hulls. It looked like the fleet had come out to greet them. But his relief

changed to alarm as the subs surged forwards and their guns swivelled to take aim.

"Uh-oh!" Niobe said.

"Wait!" Max shouted. "It's us!"

The fleet must have got ready for an invasion by Cora! It would be too cruel if they were shot down by their own side, after all they had been through.

"Max! Max!" Rivet came doggy-paddling towards them from between the subs, his metal tongue hanging out lopsidedly. The dogbot came right up to the aquabike, nudging against it.

The submarines' guns retracted.

"Phew!" Lia said.

Max reached down and patted Rivet, overjoyed to see his pet again. "Hey, Rivet – you can talk!"

"Yes Max! Got Callum! Follow!"

The dogbot began to swim upwards

towards the battleships.

"Better get my Amphibio mask back on," Lia said.

The first thing Max saw when they broke the surface was the Aquoran flagship, with his dad leaning over the rail. Max waved. "Dad! It's us!"

His dad waved back and left the rail, and a few moments later a lifeboat was let down. They climbed in and were winched up to the deck, where Callum was waiting to meet them. Spike remained in the sea, swimming along beside the ship.

Callum stood tall in his black naval uniform, the sun glinting off the gold braid and buckles. His face crinkled into a grin as they came on board. He ran forward and hugged Max, Niobe and then Lia.

"Thank Vorn you're all right! Luckily we

were patrolling this area, and we got Rivet's message," Callum said. "Strangest distress call I've ever heard – all he said was 'Sandwiches'! I guessed something was up with his speech circuits so I reprogrammed them. But what's happening – is Aquora in danger?"

"Not any more," Max said.

"But where have you been?" Callum asked.

"It's a long story," Lia said.

"In the Lost Lagoon!" Niobe said excitedly.

"What?" Callum's eyebrows shot up to his hairline. "I thought it was a myth!"

"It's real, Dad," Max said. "Come on, I'll show you the entrance."

He pulled his dad over to the ship's rail, thinking to show him the shimmering, odd-coloured portal in the sea. But there was nothing. Just the level blue water, stretching to the horizon, and Spike swimming alongside the battleship. "It's gone!" Max said.

"Maybe it changes locations," Niobe said. "What if we can't find it again?"

"Then good," Lia said. "Because I never want to go back there!"

"You'll have to tell me the whole story," Callum said. "But first let's go and get something to eat – you must be hungry after all your adventures."

He led them below deck to his cabin, a comfortable, wood-panelled room, in stark contrast to the gleaming metallic equipment around the rest of the ship. They all sat around the table. An Aquoran naval officer quickly appeared. "Could you get us something to eat, Lieutenant Spiggins?" Callum asked. The officer saluted and hurried out.

"So – how *did* you get into the Lost Lagoon?" Callum asked.

"It was some kind of portal, near my old lab," Niobe explained. "We just went there to pick up some of my old equipment. That's when we ran into Cora Blackheart..."

Lia chimed in. "But then we were swept up in a huge whirlpool, and the next moment we were in the lagoon."

Callum smiled in wonder.

"Cora followed us in," Max continued.

"She'd got hold of some of the Professor's Robobeasts," Niobe said. "And a visor to control them. But we defeated them all. Cora's still in the Lost Lagoon. The last we saw of her, she was being chased by a giant pufferfish! I don't think she'll be causing trouble any time soon."

"And we have the compass," Max said. "Still, somehow I feel like we haven't heard the last of her."

"Well, it sounds like she's quite stuck for the time being, at least," Callum said. "And the Professor's still in jail. So we can enjoy a bit of peace at last."

There was a tap at the door and Spiggins returned, carrying a huge plate.

"Sandwiches!" barked Rivet.

Max looked at the dogbot, concerned. Had his speech circuits flipped again?

Spiggins put the plate down on the table, and Max saw that it was piled high with very

tasty-looking sandwiches. Everyone laughed, and Rivet wagged his stubby iron tail.

Finally Max felt that he could relax. It was good to have his family and friends around him, knowing that Cora was still trapped in the Lost Lagoon. He knew it was too much to hope that this was the last threat to peace on Nemos. *But whatever danger faces us next,* Max thought, *we'll be ready.*

Don't miss Max's next Sea Quest adventure,
when he faces

SYTHID
THE SPIDER CRAB

Look out for all the books in
Sea Quest Series 5:

THE CHAOS QUADRANT

SYTHID THE SPIDER CRAB
BRUX THE TUSKED TERROR
VENOR THE SEA SCORPION
MONOTH THE SPIKED DESTROYER

OUT IN APRIL 2015!

Don't miss the
BRAND NEW
Special Bumper Edition:
DRAKKOS
THE OCEAN KING

978 1 40832 848 4

OUT IN NOVEMBER 2014

WIN AN EXCLUSIVE
GOODY BAG

In every Sea Quest book the Sea Quest logo is hidden in one of the pictures. Find the logos in books 13-16, make a note of which pages they appear on and go online to enter the competition at

www.seaquestbooks.co.uk

Each month we will put all of the correct entries into a draw and select one winner to receive a special Sea Quest goody bag.

You can also send your entry on a postcard to:

Sea Quest Competition, Orchard Books,
338 Euston Road, London, NW1 3BH

Don't forget to include your name and address!

GOOD LUCK

Closing Date: Nov 30th 2014

IF YOU LIKE SEA QUEST, YOU'LL LOVE **BEAST QUEST!**

FREE COLLECTOR CARDS INSIDE!

Series 1: COLLECT THEM ALL!

An evil wizard has enchanted the magical beasts of Avantia. Only a true hero can free the beasts and save the land. Is Tom the hero Avantia has been waiting for?

978 1 84616 483 5

978 1 84616 482 8

978 1 84616 484 2

978 1 84616 486 6

978 1 84616 485 9

978 1 84616 487 3

DON'T MISS THE
BRAND NEW SERIES OF:

Series 15: VELMAL'S REVENGE

978 1 40833 487 4

978 1 40833 489 8

978 1 40833 491 1

978 1 40833 493 5

COMING SOON!